A Fishy Alphabet Story

JOANNE & DAVID WYLIE

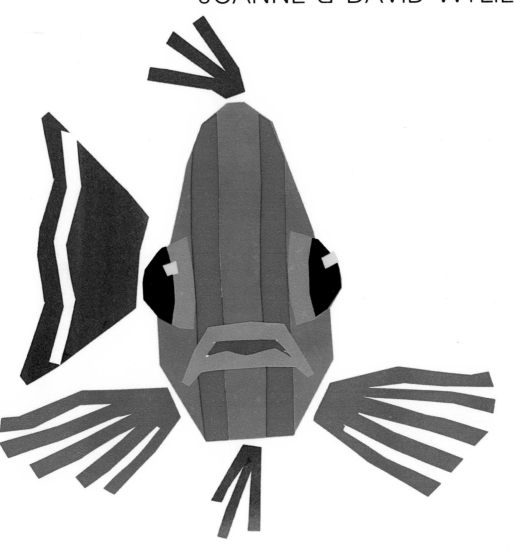

CHILDRENS PRESS™ Fishy Fish Stories®

JOANNE & DAVID WYLIE

A FISH

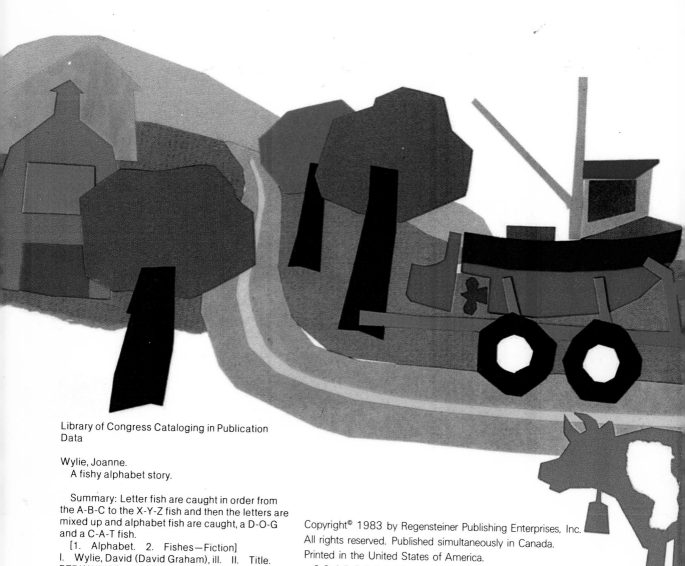

Library of Congress Cataloging in Publication
Data

Wylie, Joanne.
   A fishy alphabet story.

   Summary: Letter fish are caught in order from
the A-B-C to the X-Y-Z fish and then the letters are
mixed up and alphabet fish are caught, a D-O-G
and a C-A-T fish.
   [1. Alphabet.   2.   Fishes—Fiction]
I. Wylie, David (David Graham), ill. II. Title.
PZ7.W9775Fi 1983   [E]   83-7510
ISBN 0-516-02981-9   AACR2

ALPHABET STORY

Tomorrow I will catch some letter-fish

4

ut I must catch them in order.

My friends asked,
"What will you catch first?"
I said,

"The ABC fish."

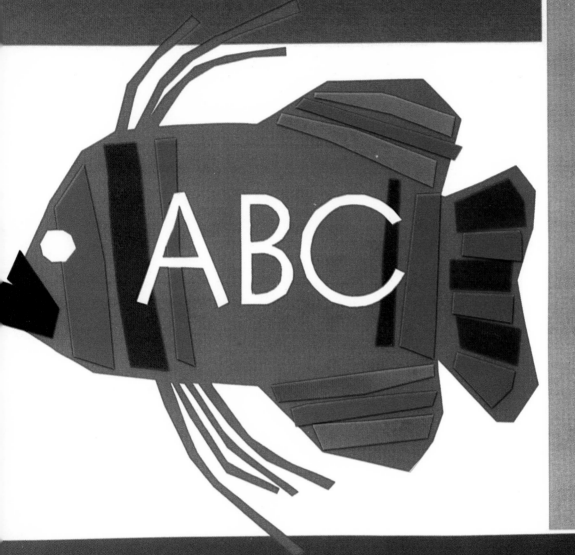

"Then after the ABC fish?"
I said,

"The DEF fish."

"Then after the DEF fish?"
I said,

"The GHI fish."

"Then after the GHI fish?"
I said,

"The JKL fish."

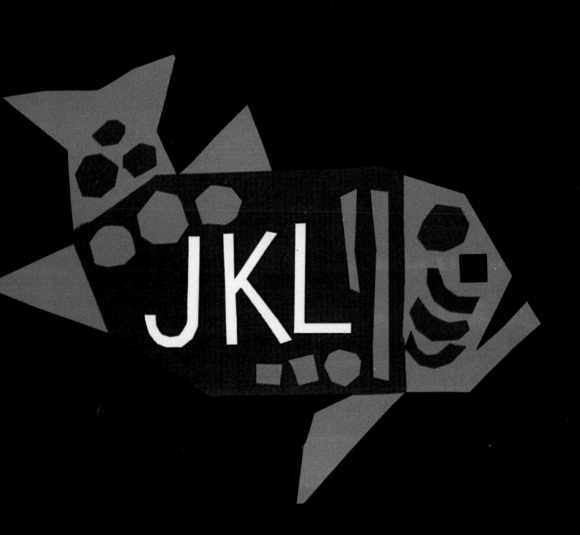

"Then after the JKL fish?"
I said,

"The MNO fish."

"Then after the MNO fish?"
I said,

"The PQR fish."

"Then after the PQR fish?"
I said,

"The STU fish."

19

"Then after the STU fish?"
I said,

"The VW fish."

"Then after the VW fish?"
I said,

"The XYZ fish."

"Then after the XYZ fish?"

I said, "I'll catch an ALPHABET fish."

Will you help me catch these fish?

WORD LIST (30 WORDS)

a	me
after	must
alphabet	my
an	order
asked	said
but	some
catch	story
first	the
fish	them
fishy	then
friends	these
help	tomorrow
I	what
in	will
letter	you

Joanne and David Wylie have collaborated on numerous workbooks, storybooks and learning materials for early childhood.

Joanne, born in Oak Park, Illinois, a graduate of Northwestern University, taught pre kindergarten, kindergarten and first grade for many years. She now devotes her time to writing materials that will help children learn to read and love to read.

David, born in Scotland, attended school in Chicago and studied art at the Art Institute and the F. B. Mizen Academy. He retired early from business and moved to the country to collaborate with his wife Joanne on a series of books for preschool and primary children.